# TO FLY

## LUCIA SCUDERI

**English text adaptation by
Phillis Gershator and Robin Blum**

A CRANKY NELL BOOK

 Kane/Miller Book Publishers

Brooklyn, New York & La Jolla, California

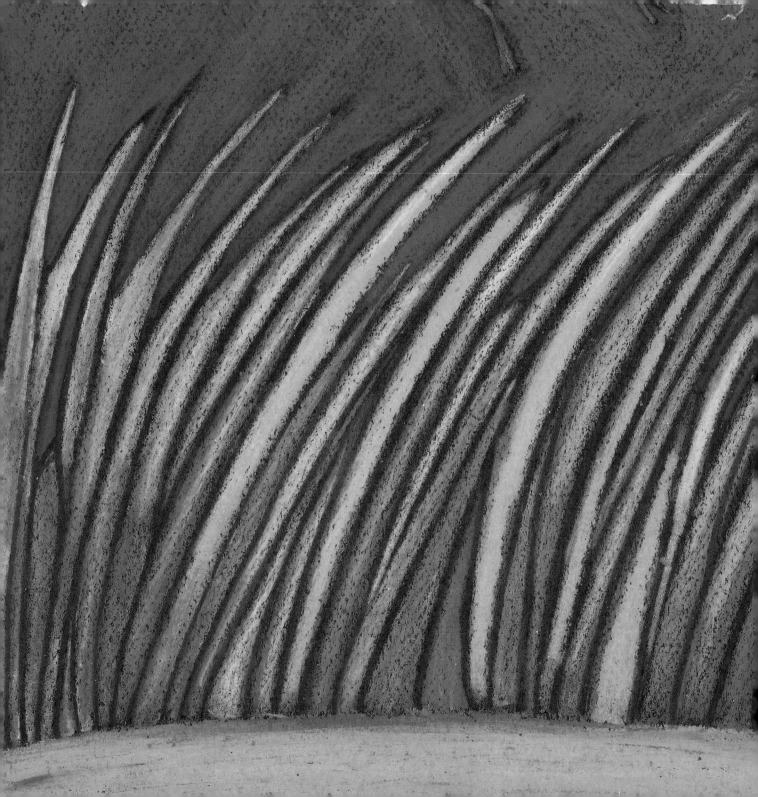

Not here!

Where?

Flap flap. Trying . . .

It's too soon . . .

for flying.

A squawk . . .

Now where?

In the air!

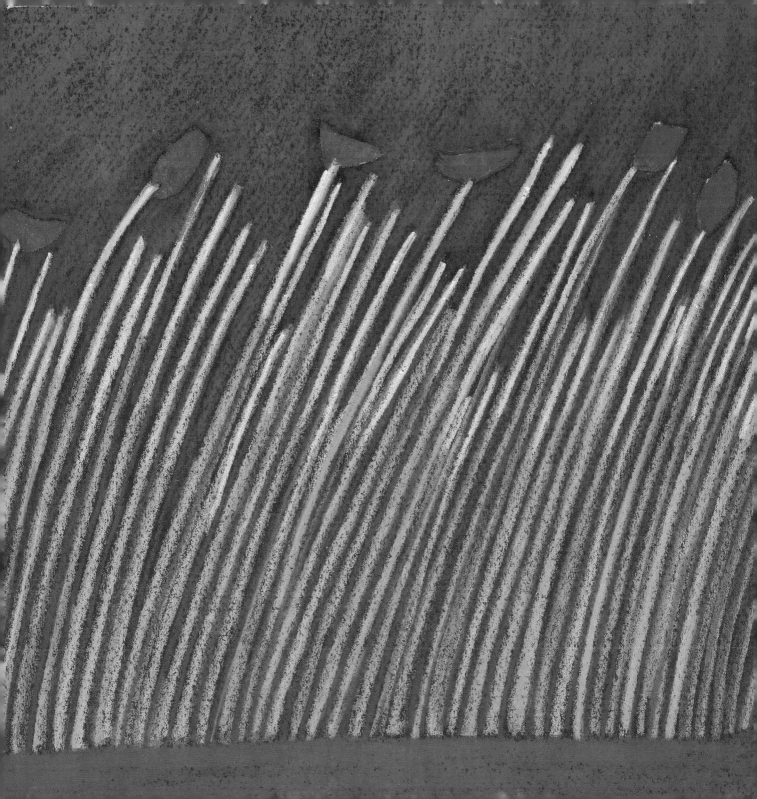

Up there!

Now's the time . . .

. . . all try

To fly!